skeleton beach

Published by

m2f publishing limited

5 Windlesham Avenue

Brighton BN1 3AH

England

Text © Bethan Christopher 2005

Illustrations © James Browne 2005

The moral right of the illustrator has been asserted

Made and printed in the EC

British Library Cataloguing in Publication Data
A CIP catalogue record for this book is available from the British Library

ISBN: 1-904948-04-9

skeleton beach

written by
Bethan Christopher

illustrated by
James Browne

monday 2 **friday books**
one story five bedtimes

m2f publishing limited

contents

Specially written for grown-ups to read
to children aged 5-8, **m2f** books help
with the bedtime routine. Each chapter
is the same length – around 10-15 minutes
reading out loud – full of fun and
adventure for you and your children to
enjoy together. Now everyone will look
forward to bedtime.

monday

Mum hammered on the door with her fist. "Jody! Get out here now!"

"No!" bellowed Jody, shoving her wooden toy box in front of the door. "I'm not leaving. You can't make me."

Hearing her mum stomp down the stairs, Jody sat down on the chest and folded her arms. The room looked horribly bare and cold now that everything was packed away in cardboard boxes. All the clay models that she had made at school (she'd displayed them on the dresser and window sill) were now wrapped in newspaper and ready for the move. The bookshelf was empty. The only thing left was her fading Spiderman duvet, heaped on the bed.

"Don't worry room," Jody whispered.

"It's not over yet."

She imagined herself sitting in here for weeks. Mum and Dad would beg and plead for her to come out, but Jody wouldn't give in. They would offer her everything: trips to Disney World, the puppy she'd always begged for, chocolate sundaes, but she wouldn't budge.

Thinking of chocolate made Jody lick her lips. They had only eaten lunch an hour ago, so she hadn't bothered to bring any food up with her. Maybe she should have brought one or two chocolate digestives. There was a whole packet in the cupboard downstairs. They happened to be her favourites.

Feeling herself weakening, Jody quickly stood up and pattered across to the window. Outside the sun was shining. On the bank, next to the museum, her big brother Alex was angrily shooting leaves

with his spud gun. His floppy hair kept
falling in his eyes and made him look like a
bad-tempered sheep dog.

"Jody?" Her heart jumped at the sound
of her dad's voice. He sounded serious.
"Get out here now."

She froze, wondering what to do. She
could tell by Dad's voice that he and Mum
meant business. They would go ape if she
stayed in here for much longer. But if she
surrendered and came out, Dinosaur
Cottage and the museum would be sold.

She would move miles away from her best mate Eleanor and have to start a whole new school. It wasn't fair.

"I'm not going!" she roared in her biggest, most ferocious voice. (It hurt her throat quite badly and she started to cry.)

Her mum and dad went quiet for a bit. Then Dad said softly, "Come out, sweetheart. Let's talk about this, eh?"

He sounded so gentle and so nice, Jody found herself heaving the toy box from the door. Slowly she opened it. Mum's face was looking a bit red. Dad looked concerned. He had been boxing up the fossils from the museum and his T-shirt was covered in dust. He knelt down and opened his arms for Jody to hug him.

"Listen, Jodes." Dad stroked her hair (which she liked even though she was nearly ten). "We have to sell the museum. Nobody wants to look at fossils now that Reptile World has opened down the road."

"Reptile World can suck eggs," muttered Jody.

All the kids at school were going on about Reptile World non-stop. There was a huge roller-coaster, shaped like a snake. Apparently it was so scary it made Jessie Parker from Year 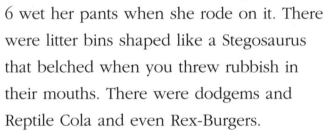 6 wet her pants when she rode on it. There were litter bins shaped like a Stegosaurus that belched when you threw rubbish in their mouths. There were dodgems and Reptile Cola and even Rex-Burgers.

Dad's fossil museum had nothing like that. There was just the converted barn that housed a bunch of yellowing fossils and the café where her mum sold scones and sandwiches.

"Is there no way we can stay?" Jody asked her dad, desperately.

"Unless a whole herd of dinosaurs walks

out of the cliff for us to display in the museum, we just can't keep Dinosaur Cottage."

"A whole herd of dinosaurs," Jody said thoughtfully. "That's what we need."

She leapt out of his arms (nearly knocking him backwards) and tore off down the stairs.

"Jody!" Her dad shouted after her.

Jody didn't hear. She ran out into the museum gardens.

"Alex, come with me!" she blurted as she hurried by her brother.

He glanced up from his spud gun and scowled. "Why should I, Chubber?"

"Because I'm going fossil hunting!"

Jody nipped into the museum. She hurried past the display cases that once held the Diplodocus poos and prehistoric sharks' teeth. Now all that stuff was in boxes, ready to be sold to a bigger, better museum.

What we need are some massive dinosaur skeletons, thought Jody. *The scariest, nastiest ever! That would make people want to come here again.*

She began rummaging through the boxes. Eventually, she found what she was looking for: her dad's fossil-hunting chisels and hammers. She snatched them up and zipped off, leaving the door banging behind her.

Outside, Alex had stopped shooting his spud gun and was loitering by the museum.

"Dad'll kill you when he finds out you've got his tools."

"So? He won't care when I've saved Dinosaur Cottage," replied Jody and marched away towards the cliff path.

"Save Dinosaur Cottage? Yeah right, Fatty. Dad says it's as good as sold. They just need to sign the last papers."

"And Dad also says that if we had some fossils – and I mean some really wicked fossils – we might be able to keep the museum. People would want to come and see them," Jody insisted.

Alex started to laugh. "That's the dumbest thing I've ever heard! You'll never find the sort of fossils Dad means. He means we need WHOLE dinosaurs, not little bits of shell and an ammonite or two."

They were at the edge of the cliff now, just where the steps began. Jody turned round. "Dad said this cliff was full of dinosaur bones. All we have to do is find them."

"It will take months. Years."

"Then you come up with a better idea," Jody snapped. "Except you can't because you're too thick."

"At least I'm not fat, Lardo!"

"Call me that again and I'm going to punch your face in," Jody shouted, as she started down the steps. Alex followed. The steps were the only way you could get down to the beach below. They were so steep and narrow, it was like picking your way down a snake's spine. Each plank was rickety and wobbled from side to side. Luckily Jody and Alex were used to running up and down them and within minutes their trainers hit the beach.

"So, where are you going to start?" Alex asked.

"Over there I guess." Jody pointed at the nearest bit of cliff.

She stamped over, crouched down and carefully held the chisel end to a boulder. With the hammer, she tapped the other end firmly. Splinters and chunks of rock began to come away, exposing the grey clay beneath. It was always such a brilliant feeling when you came upon the knuckly shape of a fossil. Almost like finding treasure.

Jody glanced over her shoulder at Alex. He didn't come and help. Instead he gazed at the beach, probably imagining another boy, from another family, looking in his rock pools for crabs and playing footie on his beach. Leaving this place felt as if your best Christmas present was being given to a kid you didn't even know!

"I wish we could stay here for ever," he said, sitting down on a rock. She watched

him pick up a stone and absently hurl it
into the water. The stone plopped behind a
wave and was gone. Alex reached down for
a second stone. This time he paused and
glanced down.

"Jody! Look what I've found!"

"What?" She was still annoyed with him
for calling her 'Fatty' and 'Lardo'.

"Just look!" yelled Alex, jumping up and
running over, shingle flying
out in every direction.

"It's a hag-stone."

He offered the stone for
Jody to see. Jody
took the rock, which
filled her palm. On
the outside it was
normal, grey and smooth.
She turned it over and
gasped.

The stone had a hole
running straight through it!

The inside was encrusted with green and yellow swirly crystal.

"If this really is a hag-stone, that means magic," she breathed. "Dad told me about them once. He said wizards used to use them."

Jody remembered walking along the cliff-top meadows and her dad telling her stories about old tunnels in the

cliffs; a wizard who lived in a cave near here and a hag-stone that made wishes come true.

"It's a shame we don't have any magical powers. If we did, we could save Dinosaur Cottage," Jody said.

Alex, curling his fingers around the hag-stone, looked round the beach – their beach – and nodded thoughtfully. "I just wish that those skeletons would come alive

and walk straight out of the rock for us,"
he said.

As he said it, a cloud passed over the sun.
Its cold shadow swallowed the beach and
the children looked up, shivering. Suddenly,
from behind them there came a deep,
rumbling groan. It sounded like a volcano
awakening inside the cliff.

Alex and Jody swung round in fright. As they watched, tiny rocks began crumbling off the cliff face, rolling and bouncing down until they hit the sand. Then, all along the cliff, great shards of rock and earth began to slide.

"LAND SLIP!" screamed Jody.

As they fled, giant lumps of rock hit the shingle, exploding into tiny stinging missiles that fired at the children's legs and arms. Only when Alex and Jody had waded out into the cold, slurping sea did they dare turn round again.

The beach was transformed. Massive slopes of rock had appeared and the air was thick with dust.

Jody's mouth dropped open. She blinked in disbelief.

"Alex, look! It can't be."

Amidst the haze and crumbled earth, towered the monstrous skeleton of a Tyrannosaurus Rex. Its time in the cliff had worn its bones bare. For a moment the dinosaur was still, pausing for the dust to fall from its ribcage. Then, the giant skull moved. It turned round and looked straight towards the children.

That's it for tonight

Sleep well. We'll find out what happens to Jody and Alex and the hag-stone next time, in Skeleton Beach.

tuesday

or whatever day
it happens to be

What happened last time?

Jody and her brother Alex live at a dinosaur fossil museum with their mum and dad, but they are being forced to move because there aren't enough tourists coming any more. Jody's dad told her that the only way they could stay is if they got a whole herd of new, exciting dinosaur skeletons. Determined not to give up her home, Jody led Alex down to the beach to look for dinosaur bones. They didn't find any bones, but Alex found a magic hag-stone, once used by witches and wizards for magic spells. He wished that all of the skeletons in the cliff would come alive. To their amazement, it really worked. In a thunderous explosion of dust, an angry looking Tyrannosaurus Rex skeleton pulled itself out of the cliff and after shaking itself free of the rocks, turned its attention to the horrified children. Now read on...

With a deafening roar, the Tyrannosaurus Rex began striding towards the children. Its tail smashed the shingle up like a great whip. The whole beach trembled.

"Swim for your life!" yelled Alex, wading out to sea.

Jody couldn't move. She stood there in the shallow water, gawping at the beach in disbelief.

"Jody!" cried Alex. His voice was distant. Jody glanced round and saw her brother thrashing around next to an orange buoy. He waved his arms and beckoned frantically. "Quickly!"

Jody splashed out towards him. As the icy water reached her chest, there was an almighty bellow from behind. The Tyrannosaurus had reached the water's edge and it began to roar and stamp as if the salty foam stung its feet. Jody didn't hang around to watch.

She dived into the water and swam as fast as she could, until she reached Alex.

On the beach everything was still a blur of red dust and rocks. The air stank of ancient soot. As the dust began to thin, Jody saw something that made the hairs on her neck go bristly.

Even more dinosaur skeletons were emerging from the cliff. Some were small and thin, but others looked bigger than JCBs. They shook themselves like giant dogs, gnashing at the air and roaring.

"Dad was right," panted Jody. "The cliff is full of dinosaur skeletons!"

"You mean was. Now they're crawling all over the beach. What are we going to do?" Alex shouted over the din.

"It started when you made the wish on the hag-stone –" began Jody. She was interrupted by a terrible noise. They turned to see an Iguanodon, as big as a truck, staggering into a bewildered Stegosaurus. The Stegosaurus let out a siren wail and the two began to fight. Meanwhile, the

Tyrannosaurus started wading out into the sea, dragging its tail through the seaweed and snapping at the waves.

Jody's heart pounded. Her legs felt like jelly.

"Hurry up and make another wish on the hag-stone," she told Alex. "You have got it, haven't you?"

From the beach there was another blood-curdling wail.

"Come on Alex!" Jody pleaded.

Alex did as he was told. He pulled the hag-stone out of his pocket.

"I wish that all the dinosaurs would be frozen on the beach," he bellowed.

Jody looked around. She sucked in a breath and waited for the sky to cloud over, for the beach to become silent again.

Nothing happened.

"I wish the dinosaurs would go back where they came from," Alex tried. He shot Jody an anxious look. Still nothing. The Tyrannosaurus Rex was so close they could see his teeth glinting. The hag-stone had to work!

"I wish the dinosaurs would go back to the cliffs!" Alex blurted out. "It's not working!"

"I can see that. What are we going to do?"

Alex peered around frantically. "The only way off the beach is up the steps. We'll never make it through all those dinosaurs!" Suddenly he stopped and stared at where the cliff met the sea. "What's that?" he spluttered.

At the far end of the cove, where the cliff had crumbled away, they could now see a tiny round cave. It definitely hadn't been there yesterday. Better still, none of the dinosaurs were near it.

Jody squinted across. She saw that the
cave was quite close to the water's edge.
Without a word, she turned and began
swimming for her life. The current dragged

and shoved her. Behind, she could hear
Alex splashing and the furious bellow of the
Tyrannosaurus as it saw them swimming
away.

Just then a huge wave crashed down onto
Jody. Her mouth and nose filled with thick
salt water. She spluttered and flailed and
pulled herself back to the surface. As she
turned her head to try and gulp in some air,
she saw the dinosaurs on the beach. There

were loads of them and they seemed to be following along the shoreline.

"Alex!" Jody snatched a glance over her shoulder.

"Just keep swimming!" yelled Alex.

Jody felt as if her arms were going to fall off her shoulders. Suddenly her knee scraped against a rock. The water was getting shallow. They had nearly made it. She put her feet down and staggered along the rocks, seaweed wrapping around her legs like rope. Now all that lay between them and the safety of the cave were some shallow rock pools and a very thin strip of shingle.

"The dinosaurs are nearly here," Alex spluttered breathlessly, behind Jody. "Don't stop! Are you ready to run?"

Jody gulped. "I think so."

"You go first," Alex said. "I'll keep an eye on them. Ready, steady..."

Jody sucked in a deep breath.

"Go!"

Jody wasn't a good runner. It came from being a bit overweight. She got a stitch within seconds of cross-country runs at school and she always came last on sports day. But when Alex shouted, "go," Jody ran like never before. The water tried to suck off her trainers; the sea-weedy rocks made her slip, yet she managed to keep going.

Within seconds she was on the shingle, scrambling into the cave and collapsing in an aching, panting heap.

Alex wasn't so lucky.

As he ran over the sludgy rocks, his foot slipped out from beneath him and he landed smack on his rear end.

"Ow!"

"Alex!" cried Jody. She gaped helplessly as Alex tried

to get up from the rock. He slipped and fell down again.

Jody watched in horrified silence as a dark shadow fell over her brother. Holding her hands over her eyes, she peeped through her fingers to see a thin, ugly, hunched-over dinosaur hovering just a few centimetres from Alex's face. It grinned. Needle-sharp teeth glinted in the sun.

"Alex!" Jody bawled. "Throw something at it!"

Alex dug a hand into his pocket. Quick as a flash, he whipped out his spud gun and opened fire on the monster.

The tiny potato bullets pinged into the skeleton's mouth. Shocked, it snapped its jaws shut

and took a few steps back. In that moment,
Alex ducked out of its way and came
zipping across the shingle towards the cliff.

Throwing down his spud gun, he used
both hands to clamber up the scree slope
and into the cave.

On the beach there was uproar. Dinosaurs
of every shape and size snapped and
gawked at the mouth of the cave. Jody and
Alex shuffled backwards further and further,
but the cave didn't seem to have an end.
They kept crawling until the light from the
hole dimmed and the
terrible noises faded.

"Alex, are you okay?"
asked Jody, clutching her brother's arm.
"I thought you were a goner."

"I would have been if it wasn't for my
spud gun," replied Alex breathlessly. His
voice echoed into the darkness.

"How far back do you think this cave
goes?" Jody asked.

"I think it's a tunnel," Alex said. "I reckon we're going uphill. We should come out sooner or later."

Sooner or later felt like hours. Jody opened her eyes and shut them but the darkness didn't change. She groped her way along, feeling the walls becoming narrower and the tunnel roof lower. Once she had to lie flat on her belly and pull herself along.

The further they went, the more worried Jody became. What if the tunnel came to a dead end and there was no way out? What if it took them right back to the beach again?

"Come on," Alex whispered after a while, "I think the tunnel is getting wider."

"Yes, it is," Jody replied. "I can crawl on

my hands and knees aga – "

Before she could finish, her nose hit something cold and damp. It made a funny crunchy noise.

"What was that?" she cried, jerking backwards and bumping her head on the roof.

"My backside," Alex growled.

"Yuk!" Jody rubbed her nose. "What's wrong? Is it a dead end?"

"Not sure. I think it's getting lighter ahead." Alex's voice sounded hopeful. "Come on."

They crawled faster and before long were able to stand up. The noises on the beach were far away now, and the darkness here didn't seem quite so thick. Jody noticed the tunnel walls getting wider until she could no longer touch them. Then, without any warning, they stopped altogether. Jody blinked. She could see the dark shape of Alex in front of her.

"Where are we?" she whispered.

Alex didn't answer at first. Everything was silent except for something dripping from the roof. Finally, he said, "We're in some sort of cave. Can you stop slinking about? You're spooking me."

Jody frowned. "I haven't moved. I'm still standing over here."

"What?" said Alex, rubbing his head. "But I just felt you moving around."

"Well, it wasn't me," Jody muttered.

"No," said a voice in the darkness, "it was me."

That's it for tonight

Sleep well. We'll find out more about Jody and Alex and the hag-stone next time, in Skeleton Beach.

wednesday

Alex's wish on a magic hag-stone brought angry dinosaur skeletons snapping out of the cliff on the beach near their house. With no escape off the beach, Jody and Alex were forced into the sea. Alex tried to make another wish on the hag-stone, but nothing happened. Then they noticed that where the cliff had slipped, a cave had been unearthed. They swam for it and just about managed to climb inside before Alex nearly got gobbled up. The cave turned out to be the entrance to a tunnel, which led to a cavern deep inside the cliff. Standing in the dark, Alex felt something brush past him. He thought it was Jody, but when he asked her, another voice replied. Someone is in the cavern with them. Now read on...

Alex swung around in the darkness. "Who was that? Jody was that you?"

"No, it's ME," boomed the same voice as before. "The Great Marvo..." There was a pause, then the voice added, "at least, I think that's who I am."

In front of them, Jody heard footsteps moving. Someone struck a match. It was still very dark, but she could just about make out the shape of an old man. He was wearing a dark robe with the hood pulled

down over his eyes.

"Am I dreaming?" he asked, holding up
the match. "Two squiggly little children in
my cave? This is very bizarre. Are you real?"

"Of course we're real," Alex said, about to
step forward. Jody grabbed his arm.

"Mum says we shouldn't talk to strangers,"
she reminded him.

The Great Marvo let out a chuckle and
scratched his head. "Hmm, well done little
girl. I see there is a fair bit of brain in that

noggin of yours. There are certainly many mucky pieces of dingledirt out there in the world. Wurglars, thieves, runkfishes, wizards of every variety..."

"There's no such thing as wizards," frowned Alex, shivering. His clothes were still damp from being in the sea and it was chilly in the cave.

"No such thing as wizards?" hooted the Great Marvo, pulling a candle from the pocket of his robe and lighting the wick. "Wizards are the reason the world goes round. Wizards are why the flowers bloom in spring time. If it weren't for wizards, the very fabric of time would tear at the hem and the world's clothes would fall off! No such thing as wizards. Pah!"

Alex wrapped his arms around himself. "Well, I've never met one."

"Probably a fortunate thing. Most of them are pearl-pinching, gold-grabbing, stone-swizzeling rotstinkers."

As he talked, the Great Marvo pulled more and more candles out of his pocket. Where were they all coming from? Jody watched, awestruck, as he shuffled around the cave, arranging candles on rocky ledges and lighting them with his match.

"Are you a wizard?" she asked nervously.

"The very greatest!" the Great Marvo shouted proudly. "Well, I was

before that miserable Norfin d'Loof stole my best magic." He paused and turned to the children.

"Which reminds me, how did you get into this cave? That tunnel has been blocked for years."

"It was," Jody said. "But there was a massive landslip on the beach. Loads of dinosaur skeletons started coming out of the cliff. The entrance to the tunnel opened up and we escaped just in time."

"Landslips? Skeletons?" murmured the Great Marvo thoughtfully. "It seems as though there is some strange magic afoot."

Suddenly Jody was filled with relief that they had found this old man.

"Can you show us the way out of here, Mr Marvo?" she asked. "We've got to tell our mum and dad what's happened before

anyone goes to the beach and gets hurt."

The old man turned away slowly and hung his head. "I'm afraid there isn't any other way out, little girl. Believe me. The only way out of here is back down the tunnel."

Jody turned and glanced at the tunnel entrance. It didn't make sense.

"But, you said the tunnel has been blocked up for years. If that is the only way out, how did you get here?"

The Great Marvo turned, shuffled over to a large piece of rock and sat down.

"You don't want to know how I got in here, my squiggly pet." His shoulders slumped.

Jody leant slowly forward.

"Yes, I do," she said kindly.

"You have to tell us, if we are going to get out of here," added Alex.

The Great Marvo nodded. "You're right. But you must remember, I am a kind, good wizard. I was the greatest magic-maker of my time. People flocked to me for brews and conjurations. Nobody was scared of me. I was greatly respected."

Jody nodded.

"But I wasn't the only wizard out there, you see. It's a very sought after profession, is wizardry. Magic-hungry scoundrels tried all sorts of tricks to learn my magic. Wurglars stole into my house –"

"You mean burglars?"

"That's what I said! Thieving thumberwubs stole my things when I was out visiting friends. In the end I took to living in this very cave, just to protect my secrets and charms."

"But one day, a particularly sneaky wizarding creeper, Norfin d'Loof, slipped in here while I was sleeping. He stole my most important possession, the very core of my magical magicking. And he used its power to block up my tunnel with boulders. The only magic I had left were silly tricks – like making candles appear out of nowhere." He lit a final candle, sighing.

"I couldn't escape from this cave and nobody ever saw me again."

"But that's horrible!" cried Jody. "What a nasty piece of work. I hate that Norfin d'Goof!"

The Great Marvo nodded sadly.

"But wait a minute," said Alex. "If the tunnel was blocked and it's the only way out, that means..."

The Great Marvo nodded gravely. "I lived out my last days in this cave."

Very slowly he lifted up his arm and tugged back the sleeve of his robe.

In the candlelight, Jody saw that his hand wasn't pink and wrinkly like that of an old man, but white and thin as bone.

For a moment she felt her whole body go hot. Her heart started thumping at a hundred miles per hour, yet she couldn't move. She was frozen to the spot. She thought the Great Marvo was a nice old man, but under his robe he was just, he was just – a skeleton!

"I'm sorry," cried the Great Marvo, pulling his hand back into his sleeve. "I didn't want to show you. I knew you would be scared!"

Jody opened her mouth, but no words came out.

"That's what I meant when I said there was strange magic afoot," the wizard babbled on. "You said skeletons came out of the cliff and that must have been when I came alive too. But why? How? I'll be sniggle-flapped if I know." And with that he slumped down on a rock, as if the very thought of it had tired him out.

pages to go tonight

8

9

Jody swallowed hard. Should she tell him?

"We know why it happened," she said slowly.

Alex glared at her but she carried on. "It happened when we found the hag-stone."

The Great Marvo sat bolt upright. "You found a hag-stone?"

Jody nodded. "Yes. Alex made a wish on it. He wished all the skeletons in the cliff would come back to life. He tried to make another wish afterwards but nothing happened."

The Great Marvo jumped to his feet. "Tell me quickly. Did this hag-stone have a green and yellow crystal with a little swirl that looks like a snake running through it?"

"Yes," Alex and Jody said at once.

They stared in surprise as the old man jumped in the air and began whooping with joy. "Norfin d'Loof must have lost my stone! Norfin d'Loof must have lost my stone! You

know what this means you wondersome,
splendid children?"

Jody smiled.

"That you can magic the dinosaurs away?"

"Of course, of course, but more
importantly than that."

"What?" Jody asked, transfixed.

"Norfin d'Loof lost his power! Do you
know how many nights I sat in this
soppingly, clamtiferous cave thinking about

the magic he might have been doing and all the time the fool dropped it on the way out!" Marvo stopped dancing and let out a huge laugh.

"Alex has still got it. Would you like to have a look?"

"Yes, quickly. Give it to me!" The Great Marvo held out his bony hand. He was shaking with excitement.

Alex didn't move. "Come on, boy," the old man laughed. "Give me the hag-stone and I will be the true Great Marvo once more. We'll get you out of this cave. We'll stop those dimbly-dozy-sores. Just give me the hag-stone!"

"Go on Alex," urged Jody, "it's our only chance."

Narrowing his eyes, Alex dug a hand into his pocket and slowly drew out the hag-stone. The Great Marvo hobbled forward and took it from Alex's palm. Jody heard him whispering under his breath. He was chanting some strange language. Then, suddenly he threw up his hands and yelled, *"Spindle-mizzen!"*

There was a blast of light. The cavern lit up. It was as if someone had flicked on a light switch. The Great Marvo swung round and pulled back his hood.

Jody stepped back in surprise and gawped at the Great Marvo. In front of her stood, not a skeleton but a tall, elderly man.

Even more amazing was the size of his nose! It looked as if it had been modelled out of playdough and stuck rather badly between his eyes. Out of the bottomless nostrils coiled a jet-black moustache that twisted over his top lip like a sleeping serpent.

"Well?" said the Great Marvo, running a hand over his bald head. "Now do you believe in wizards?"

That's it for tonight

Sleep well. We'll find out more about Jody and Alex and the hag-stone next time, in Skeleton Beach.

thursday

or whatever day
it happens to be

What happened last time?

Jody and Alex, hiding from the dinosaur skeletons in a cavern, discovered that they were not alone. The Great Marvo, a skeleton wizard, was also there, but how did he get in? He explained that he had been trapped in the cave for years – ever since his enemy Norfin d'Loof stole his magical stone and blocked up the tunnel. The children gave him back the hag-stone and in a flash of magic, Marvo turned himself from the skeleton into the little old man he once was. But is he magical enough to deal with the dinosaurs who are prowling in front of the tunnel entrance? Now read on...

The Great Marvo grinned at the children from his new human face. "You have saved me, my squiggly little pets and now I will do everything I can to help you. But first things first. I'm going to conjure us a feast you'll never forget!"

"A feast?" whooped Jody. "Yes please! I think tea must have been hours ago!"

Alex frowned at Jody, and then shook his head.

"It's very nice of you thinking about giving us some food, Mr Marvo," he said politely, "but I think we should go straight

back to the beach and sort out the
dinosaurs."

The Great Marvo looked surprised.
"What's the wiggling rush?" he demanded.
"I've only just got my body back and I'm
starving. This is a time for celebration.
These dingle-dimple-sores aren't that
dangerous, are they?"

"Yes they are," Alex,
shouted, remembering
the beach.

Just talking about the
dinosaurs was enough to
put Jody off any thoughts of food.

"They're man-eaters!" she said.
"I thought everyone knew that. We learnt
about dinosaurs in reception class. They
have great big teeth."

"Shh!" hissed Alex suddenly, "I think I
heard something in the tunnel."

Jody listened. At first it sounded like
scratching and stones clattering on the floor.

"Maybe it's Mum and Dad," whispered Jody. "They've come to look for us."

She stopped dead as a terrible screech blasted out of the tunnel and echoed through the cave.

"A dinosaur," Alex gulped. "It's coming this way. Quickly, move back!"

Jody and the Great Marvo hurried over to where Alex was already against the wall. The noise was getting louder and louder. It sounded like a wooden chair being thrown down some steps, clattering and snapping as it went.

Jody stared at the gaping tunnel mouth and suddenly, out of it came a giant skeleton bird. It wasn't flying, but its wings were trying to. The clattering noise came from its bones hitting the stone floor.

"A Pterodactyl!" Alex stared at the huge

creature as it rattled into the cavern.

"A baby Pterodactyl."

"Baby?" exclaimed the Great Marvo, holding up the hag-stone. "If that's a baby, I'd hate to meet its mum."

The Pterodactyl turned then. Its hollow eyes surveyed the huddled trio and its long, sharp beak snapped open.

"Do something, Mr Marvo!" shrieked Jody.

"Minglemort and cackling crone," shouted the wizard. *"Turn this beast into stone. Ziggley-zoot!"*

Jody watched as a flash of blue light flew out of the hag-stone and hit the Pterodactyl. For a moment the skeleton was lit up like some strange, bird-like sculpture, then the light was gone and everything fell silent.

Jody stared at the frozen Pterodactyl. "You did it."

"That was a close call," Alex sighed. "Now can we go to the beach before anything else happens?"

The Great Marvo stepped forward, staring at the Pterodactyl. He gave it a little prod, and then turned to Alex.

"You're right, boy. There is no time for celebrations. We've got work to do."

The Great Marvo gave them each a candle and led them into the tunnel. To begin with it was easy to walk, but after a while the walls pulled tighter and the roof sloped low. Further down the tunnel, echoed the sound of roaring and gnashing cries. The thought of seeing all the dinosaurs again made Jody's legs feel like jelly.

"Mr Marvo?" she shouted over Alex's shoulder. "What will we do if the hag-stone doesn't work?"

"The hag-stone fail to work, my squiggly pet?" came the Great Marvo's muffled voice. "Of course it will work!"

"It didn't before," Alex reminded him. "When I tried to wish on it the second time, nothing happened."

The Great Marvo started to laugh. "Well, of course it didn't! Where do you think the rhyme comes from?"

"What rhyme?" Alex asked.

"Wizards and witches may wish on the stone, for ordinary folk, it's just one wish alone," Marvo chanted happily. "Don't they teach you anything any more?"

Jody was going to explain that things might have changed since he was at school (whenever that was), but the ever-closer snarls of the dinosaurs made her too scared to speak. Minutes later they emerged into

the cave above the beach and edged
gingerly towards the entrance.

Outside it was dark.
The moon had risen
and the sky was studded
with stars. Moving
around the rocks were
several monstrous, black shapes. The sheer
size of them was enough to make you feel
dizzy. Jody watched as a Diplodocus
wandered nearby. She could see the
moonlight gleaming through the gaps in its
giant ribcage. There were others nearer the
cliff and one on the edge of the sea.

The Great Marvo shook his head as if he
didn't believe what his eyes were telling him.

"I've never seen such tremendously ogglesome brutes in all my life! How many are there?"

"I can see nine altogether," whispered Alex quickly. "Come on Mr Marvo! We're wasting time."

"Are you sure there are nine? It's very important you know."

Jody counted too. "Nine," she agreed.

The Great Marvo nodded and rearranged himself so he was sitting cross-legged in the middle of the cave. He took out the hag-stone, cupped it in his hands and then in a deep voice, began to chant.

"Beasts of old, our bards once told, of your prison in the land,

But ancient stones, stir ancient bones and your feet now walk the sand.

Nine brutes of bone freeze like stone! Nine brutes of bone become like stone! Grimsfelder-Minglezink!"

There was a flash of light... everything went silent. The sea lapped at the shore.

Jody peeled her hands from her face. Had the Great Marvo's spell worked? Was it all over?

She peered over Alex's shoulder. On the beach all around stood the dinosaur skeletons, frozen exactly as they had been standing. The moonlight curled around their bones, making them gleam like silver. It looked beautiful but scary.

"Did it work?" whispered Alex, who still had his eyes tightly shut.

"Yes," breathed Jody, "it worked."

Very slowly, the three climbed out of the cave and down the scree slope. At first they stood and stared, but then Alex got brave and started creeping down the beach towards the Diplodocus skeleton. Its ribcage alone was the size of a mobile classroom. Jody watched her brother as he reached out and touched a bone. He let out a whoop and spun around, waving his arms in the air. "We did it!"

"Ah," sighed the Great Marvo, sniffing loudly and flexing his shoulders. "How good it feels to exercise some magic after a hundred years."

Jody stared around. She wasn't sure what it was, but something didn't feel quite right. She counted the dinosaur skeletons again. Like Alex said, there were nine of them. The more peaceful ones had their heads down as they searched for plants. The ferocious, man-eaters were frozen as they fought and gnashed at each other.

A frown crept across Jody's forehead.

"Wait a minute..." she whispered.

Suddenly it dawned on her. Where was the Tyrannosaurus Rex?

"Alex, come back!" screamed Jody. "There were ten dinosaurs, not nine!"

Jody's voice was drowned out by a roar that shook her to her bones. She swung round. Her whole body seemed to shrivel, for there standing right behind her was the Tyrannosaurus Rex. Its jaws were slightly open, showing rows of pointed teeth.

"Get out of the way, girl!" bellowed the Great Marvo. "Run!"

He stood his ground. Holding up the hag-stone, he started his spell.

"You brute of bone freeze like stone! You brute of bone..."
But he was too slow.
The dinosaur was
on him.

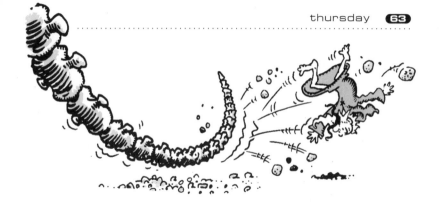

Just then, Jody remembered the spud gun.
She glanced around frantically, but it was
nowhere to be seen. Instead she grabbed a
handful of stones and hurled them at the
great brute. They clattered off its bones and
it swung round. As it did, its ten-tonne tail
smacked into the wizard and sent him
flying across the shingle.

The Great Marvo landed in a heap of
seaweed. He didn't move. Jody willed him
to get up, but he just lay like a puppet
whose strings had been cut.

The Tyrannosaurus Rex let out a satisfied
grunt. It shut it jaws, turned round and
took a step towards the boulder where
Jody was hiding.

Jody shrank down. She listened, terrified, as the dinosaur moved closer, gnashing and snorting as if trying to catch her smell on the breeze. It was so close that Jody could see its breath on the air. She hugged herself tightly, trying to become as small as she could. Then finally, after what seemed like ages, the Tyrannosaurus let out a sharp wailing sound and turned, crashing away towards the beach steps.

Jody felt her body go limp. *We're safe*, she thought. *Safe for now. But without Marvo's magic, how on earth are we going to get off this beach?*

That's it for tonight

Sleep well. We'll find out what happens to Jody and Alex and the hag-stone next time, in the final part of Skeleton Beach.

friday

or whatever day
it happens to be

Using the hag-stone, the Great Marvo transformed himself from a skeleton into a sweet old wizard. His first task was to deal with a baby Pterodactyl skeleton that clattered into the cave. With a great flash, he turned it into stone, and then he, Alex and Jody headed down the tunnel to take on the rest of the skeleton dinosaurs. Marvo did another great spell and froze all the ranting dinosaur skeletons, but he'd missed one! The Tyrannosaurus Rex lunged at him, knocking him flying and started to roam the beach looking for the children. Now read the final part of Skeleton Beach…

Jody could see Alex down by the frozen Diplodocus skeleton. He was peeping out from behind the massive tail, watching the monstrous Tyrannosaurus as it thrashed across the shingle.

What were they going to do? The only way to stop the last dinosaur was to use the hag-stone, but the Great Marvo still wasn't

moving and he was the only one who knew
how to use it.

"How is he?" Alex panted, as he ran up
behind her. He gawped at the prone figure.
"Come on Marvo, we need your rhyming
magic now. Please!"

Suddenly, Jody remembered something.

"Alex, how did the rhyme about the
stone go? Wasn't it something about
'ordinary folk get one go alone', or
something like that?"

Alex turned on his sister. "Great idea.
Let's have a poetry class while that thing's
still on the loose." He pointed down the
beach. The Tyrannosaurus Rex was staring
back at them.

"Quick. Find the stone," Jody hissed.
"You've used your wish, but I haven't had
one yet. I've got a wish too!"

Jody grabbed Marvo's hands but there
was nothing there.

A groan came from the heap of cloth.

Jody sighed in relief. "Thank goodness you're alive! Where's the hag-stone, Mr Marvo?"

"I must have dropped it," he wheezed.

Jody turned and looked at the beach. The landslide had left the whole place littered with stones and rubble. She would never be able to find it in just the moonlight.

"We've got to find the hag-stone!" Jody cried. She clambered over the rocks and groped in the rubble, tossing aside chunks of chalk and bits of flint. The rocks gashed and grated her skin, whilst the ground beneath her throbbed with the weight of the approaching dinosaur.

Suddenly, the mashing crunching stopped. Towering above them, blotting out the stars, lurked the monstrous skull of the Tyrannosaurus Rex.

"Duck!" Alex bawled.

Jody let herself fall flat against the rocks.
She felt the air brush her neck as the
gaping jaws swung down to snatch her up.
She twisted round, about to scramble away,
but then stopped dead.

"Alex!"

One of the
dinosaur's needle-sharp
teeth had snagged Alex's
T-shirt. Now he was being
lifted, high into the air,
hanging from nothing but his
top. The Tyrannosaurus Rex let out a
shattering howl.

"Jody!" Alex screamed, waving his arm
and pointing. "The hag-stone is down by
that boulder! I saw it!"

Jody swung round. She half ran, half
staggered to the place that Alex's wildly
swinging hand seemed to be pointing to
and stared desperately at the sea of stones.

Behind her, the Tyrannosaurus Rex went berserk. Like a dog with a toy, it shook its head wildly, trying to dislodge the thing hanging from its tooth. Alex was tossed and waggled like a rag doll. Much longer and every bone in his body would be broken. Suddenly, a glint of crystal caught her eye. "The hag-stone!"

"I can't remember the rhyme," she screamed.

"You don't need one," Alex yelled. "Just wish on it!"

Holding the hag-stone up to the dinosaur, in a trembling voice, she said, "I wish the T. Rex would turn to stone!"

It was as if someone had pressed 'pause'. Everything stopped. The dinosaur froze, its gaping jaws still wide open. Jody's heart stopped beating. Her breath halted in her throat. A second passed.

Then everything came to life. Everything, that is, except the dinosaur. The sea rushed, Jody's breath slid out, she saw Alex swinging slowly where he hung.

"I think I'm going to be sick," he called weakly. "That ride would beat anything at Reptile World!"

Jody let out a shaky laugh. "Are you hurt?"

"No, just dizzy," Alex answered. "What about Mr Marvo?"

Jody stumbled across to the Great Marvo. "Are you okay, Mr Marvo?"

The old wizard sat up painfully. "Yes, I think so, squiggler. Thought I was about to be squished by that dragon for a moment. You did fantastically."

Jody blushed and looked down.

"I think you would make a very good wizard, Jody," the Great Marvo went on.

"Perhaps one day I'll come back and teach you."

"Magic is too dangerous for me," Jody replied, passing the hag-stone back to its owner.

The Great Marvo took it and pointed it at Alex. *"Hold this squiggler safe and sound. Restore him to the earthly ground. Ziggle-wiggle."*

This time there wasn't a flash of light. Instead, some strange, invisible force lifted Alex up, unhooked his T-shirt and lowered him slowly onto the shingle.

From somewhere far away, Jody thought she heard her name being called. She turned round. Blue lights were flashing on the cliff top. People were waving and shouting.

"It's the police," said Alex, standing up.

"And look! There's Mum and Dad!"

"You had better go," the Great Marvo croaked.

Jody looked up at him quickly. "You're coming, aren't you?"

The old man shook his head. "Those dino dasterlies have quite worn me out. Another time perhaps?"

"What will you do?" asked Jody urgently. She could see her mum and dad scrambling down the ruined steps, still waving and calling.

"I've got plenty of things to do," said the Great Marvo, patting Jody's head. "Who else is going to stitch together the fabric of time and keep the world's clothes from falling off?" He clutched the hag-stone to his chest and began to chant in a low voice. Jody glanced at the steps. Her mum and dad were just reaching

the beach now. She turned back to the
Great Marvo and he gave her a massive
wink.

"Palmerlee-Zinglemorf!"

There was flash of light and he was gone.

"Jody! Alex! Didn't you hear us calling?"
cried their mum, running down towards
them. She held out her arms. Moments later
their dad was there too, wrapping his arms
around them and hugging them tightly.
He was followed by a couple of stunned
looking policemen.

"I've never seen anything like it..." began the policeman with glasses. Gawping at the dinosaurs, he took off his helmet and shook his head in disbelief. His radio crackled, but he ignored it.

"I don't know how you've done this," breathed Dad, gazing at the statues on the beach, "but I've got a feeling you two are lucky to be alive."

The next day, Jody didn't wake up until two in the afternoon. In the kitchen, she could hear Alex and her mum talking loudly. There were other voices too. Climbing groggily out of bed, Jody went downstairs.

The front door was open. Outside, loads of cars and vans were parked. People in suits, with cameras and notepads were milling around looking very excited. There was even one man with sunglasses and a big, black tripod and filming equipment.

Her dad was talking to him and pointing at the cliff path.

"What's going on?" Jody asked, hurrying into the kitchen. "Why didn't someone wake me up?"

Mum and Alex were sitting at the table, talking to a lady reporter.

Alex jumped up and grabbed a chair for Jody.

"Here's the hero," Alex shouted, and all of a sudden the room was full of people hurling questions.

"Are these the tools that started the landslip, Jody?" one asked, holding up her dad's fossil hammer and chisel.

"Did you know you were on to a dinosaur burial site right from the start?" shouted another.

Alex laughed at her bemused expression and she shoved him out into the hall.

"Hero? What's going on Alex?"

"Well, I couldn't tell them about hag-stones

and wizards could I? And it did all happen because you insisted on fossil hunting, didn't it?" He smiled at her. "And you did save my life, didn't you?"

He steered her back into the busy room. It was like a dream. Jody couldn't decide what was most amazing – all the reporters or the idea that her big brother was being nice to her.

"Everyone has come to see our dinosaur skeletons!" Alex cried. "Isn't that wicked? It's hitting the headlines. There's even someone from the TV here to film them."

"We're going to be on telly?" Jody asked, suddenly feeling very awake.

"Dinosaur Cottage is going to be famous," smiled the lady reporter. "You'll have

people coming from all over the world to see your collection."

Jody turned to her mum. "Does that mean we'll be allowed to stay at Dinosaur Cottage?"

"Darling!" said her mum, starting to laugh. "Of course we'll be staying!"

The lady reporter was right. Hordes of tourists from all over the world came to gaze at the collection of skeletons at Dinosaur Cottage. They murmured at the colossal size of the Diplodocus and gasped at the furious look on the face of the Tyrannosaurus. Mum had to build an extension on the café and all of Jody's friends wanted her to take them fossil hunting on the beach.

For Jody, there was just one thing missing: Marvo.

She and Alex went back to the cave but the tunnel roof had fallen in. Where had he gone? She couldn't help hoping that she

would see him again some time. She often found herself wondering what it would be like to be a real wizard, to hold together the fabric of the world and possibly conjure cakes from thin air.

Maybe one day the Great Marvo would come back and visit them. One day.

Then what happened?

If you would like to know what happened when Marvo did come back, look up m2fbooks.com on the Internet and use this special password in the password area: MARVO